ALASKA STORIES

ALASKA STORIES

by JOHN MITCHELL

Plover Press • Wasilla, Alaska • 1984

Plover Press
P.O. Box 874883
Wasilla, AK 99687

To Margo

Contents

Preface

Just because a man is born of woman or made of clay doesn't mean he is either destined or designed to fit comfortably on earth. Countless species have perished because of their unwillingness or inability to adapt, and for a while my own survival was much in doubt.

My point of departure was to take what I had read or heard in music or even witnessed in the form of fragmentary human actions – the stories form such studies – and try to find a physical context where such values could live consistently. It was the classical case of whether Mahomet should go to the mountain or it should come to him, and in my mind there wasn't much doubt which it should be.

At age eighteen, having come to view the Lower Forty-Eight as a trap where man had sold his soul for creature comforts, I set out for Alaska, which I visualized as a frozen landscape covered with igloos and somehow pure. Although the woods around Cordova, where I worked for the Forestry, bore little resemblance to the landscape I expected and the Service certainly had its share of bureaucratic ways, there were certain redeeming features. Our chief had spent his youth in the Klondike searching for gold. As a part-time reporter for the *Cordova Times*, I heard the mayor stand up against the local clergy in favor of prostitution. Alaska was a place where a man could be free.

Lacking the skills, and perhaps the mental toughness which I saw in people all around me, I made the practical concession of returning to college for five quarters. Then I took a job teaching in the Aleutians, accompanied by my wife, Margo, who had somehow been convinced to join me in this experiment. I would feel more guilty about my classroom performance if children ever learned anything in school anyway. Someone has said we learn best through adversity, conflict, bafflement; and if that is true, then the year on Sanak Island could not have been a complete loss. Margo's students learned to read, and at least mine had the practice of writing compositions. I assigned many in the hopes of finding out more about the people.

The reason my tenure in the schoolhouse didn't last was not that I was fired, but I objected to the barrier that authority always poses. I wanted to belong to the people, to learn their ways, which seemed truer than mine, but from which I was barred by the student-teacher relationship. An opportunity soon presented itself in the form of commercial fishing, and I took it. Behold, the miracle! It was not a full miracle, maybe, but certainly part of one. All at once I was receiving double what I had been paid for listening to the sound of my own voice, and I was enjoying it. Also fishing defied the principle on which I had been brought up, which was that money doesn't grow on trees. It was everywhere in the water, like manna.

In some ways herring and salmon fishing still fulfills this promise. Not only is it a way of accomplishing in the summer months what I had started out to do in nine – and most men do in eleven – it is a poor man's yachting. There is probably no fisherman in the fleet who has not at some time cursed his cannery superintendent up and down and seen this captain of industry come crawling back. As another philosopher said, "Money talks." That there are disadvantages in trusting to nature is seen in such stories as "The Corinthians," where the salmon failed, and in "Bride of the Fleet," which also describes the psychological strains inherent in being cooped up with other men on a boat. Probably my solution would not work for everybody, but I came to the fishery with a childhood spent on pleasure boats in Balboa Bay, California. I was at home on the water.

Alaska Stories can be read as crucial experiences in each of the characters' lives or as an abstraction of the itinerary which my search for survival took. "The Corinthians" is not just a fishing story, but a backward glance at a society as deadly to me as the defoliated world was to the dinosaur. Love, too, was an integral part of my vision, but some of its problems are foreshadowed in "Bride of the Fleet." Although the only apparent link between "The Compleat Moose Hunter" and my personal history is the teaching scene, I think it is also possible to read it as an early stage in that desperate passage we are already familiar with. At least I know the attitudes of the dirt-poor homestead boy bear a close similarity to my own. It is also significant that at the end he gives up the battle for individuality, having been effectively starved out, and so brings us closer to that conclusion which I think is part of the learning experience for all rebels. There is no escape.

In "Old Man Winter" we go further down the road to conformity, for although there is still wildly antisocial behavior in the form of the drunken web man, it is no longer a state our viewpoint character approves of. By "Whitemare" he has dropped to a part-time resident.

John Mitchell

ALASKA
STORIES

The Corinthians

In Puget Sound, unlike Alaska, all gillnetting for salmon is done at night. The boats light the far end of the net with a lantern, or "jack," as they used to be called – usually a kerosene lantern strapped to an inflated innertube. They were very tricky to handle, for the least wake could turn one upside down, not only putting out the flame, but cracking the glass, which had grown warm during the brief time the wick was lit on deck. Although my father was born in the Seattle area, his salmon fishing experience was all in the free and easy daylight of Alaskan waters. He dreaded having to join a fleet whose lights challenged the magnitude of Seattle's, but that year we had no choice. The Alaska salmon run had failed.

Another problem we had was getting lost. Our rented gillnetter was not equipped with a fathometer, much less with modern instrumentation such as radar or Loran C, and it was very hard to tell where you were in the Straits of Juan de Fuca, especially as regards the dividing line between the United States and Canada. To escape the crowd he'd decided to fish out of Port Angeles, and every afternoon just before dark we'd start out in a group of twenty or thirty boats. They were all in radio communication as they sampled here and there with their nets, whereas with us it was just a case of hit and miss. Except for occasional messages overheard on the radio, we might as well have been on a different planet.

"Hey, Nels!" a voice would blurt in our pilothouse, shadow-lit by its various gauges, "better wind that net in fast! I see a tanker coming down the pike about the size of the Dexter Horton Building!"

"Don't worry, I'm just putting on my boots."

"Well, don't stop to take no crap . . ."

Contrary to custom in Alaska, where rendering assistance is a way of life, the fishermen of Puget Sound ignored us completely. This surprised me. Not my father, or Harold, as I called him. He

claimed this area had always been like that. The fact
that some of these men took advantage of our hos-
pitality up North, but utterly failed to reciprocate
here, was what had propelled him onto the Last
Frontier to begin with.

At the same time, insecurity bred a desire for
pleasure, in both of us, and it wasn't long before we
established the habit, once the troublesome problem of setting the jack was solved, of going below
for a big bowl of cereal heaped with sugar and
flooded with evaporated milk. The pause took the
place of the evenings we were used to having on
our Alaskan homestead. Because of travel costs, my
mother and brother and two sisters had stayed up
North, where Harold's goal was merely to subsist.

"You know all it takes to make a good commercial fisherman?" he said, one night when we got further lost than usual.

I didn't answer, trying to pattern my behavior
on that of my mother, who was an excellent listener.
You had to be with him. He would fly off the handle
at the least untoward remark and was, it now
appears, fighting a battle which had nothing to do

with my own experience. Although my grand-parents lived only a few miles from where we tied up on weekends, he utterly refused to see them. He said he didn't want me exposed to their artificiality.

"Above average intelligence and a background in athletics. I'll bet you didn't know I played foot-ball in high school, did you, Cricket?"

"No, I didn't." His background was full of sur-prises, chiefly because he so rarely admitted its exis-tence. It was only since we'd arrived in the Sound that I'd learned he used to race Olympic Snowbirds in fancy regattas.

"Well, I did. I wasn't much good, but I enjoyed the physical contact, making tackles and throwing blocks. My life was pretty soft in those days. I remember getting on my bicycle and just riding to see if I could break out of the atmosphere. It wasn't just topography, it was pretenses. Take my first efforts to earn money. I was going to Sunday school, being dragged there every weekend against my will. I hated losing time indoors, but the choir director offered me fifty cents a week if I would sing for him, and I decided to accept. My parents had a fit! They took the attitude church was no longer important and I better get out in the air among normal boys. Can you believe it?"

Now his expression grew thoughtful, as though they still might be exercising some subtle influence. Actually there was a noise I didn't recognize. It sounded like shipworms boring into the hull.

"What do you suppose it is?" he said. "We're too far out to have run aground, aren't we?"

Before I could answer, the sound increased dramatically, and we both hurried out on deck to be met with an unusual sight. The net was being drawn under the keel with freight-train force, while all around us foam and beaver cuttings danced in a kind of marine Walpurgisnacht. Even more surprising, our net was not alone. Another was plastered to it as though inanimate objects had not only come to life here in the Straits of Juan de Fuca, but were actually breeding! Not twenty-five yards away another boat was spotting its way toward us, the beam striking the white, slug-like bodies of salmon which had sewn our nets together.

"I think I can get everything back but my jack!"

the other skipper called. "Just throw it off on the dock in the morning, will you?"

"Sure," said Harold. Then he paused. The man's accent had sounded strange. "What dock?"

"Why, Steveston!" There was another pause, as though Harold had committed some kind of social gaff. Then the other skipper shined his light right in our faces. "Say, what are you, a Yank?"

"You better believe I am!"

"Well, you're in Canada, mate, and if you don't get your ass out of here, I'm going to call the cutter and have you arrested in the name of the Queen!"

Despite the handicap of poor equipment and inexperience, we were succeeding in our essential purpose, which was to catch enough fish to see us through another Alaskan winter. Also we were doing it in spite of some unseasonably warm water temperatures which were causing the bulk of the late Adams River run to pass through Johnstone Strait and down into the Gulf of Georgia, avoiding American waters entirely. The result was we were forced out from the comparative safety of the

Salmon Banks to Cape Flattery, where the Pacific Ocean was added to the hazards of fog and steamers we were already experiencing. As if Harold's prejudice had finally taken flower, I grew seasick almost every night.

"Maybe it's the chlorine in the water," I said one morning after an exceptionally rough period outside Neah Bay. I had chosen this excuse with some care, fairly sure it could not be used against me when I got back to the homestead. Harold's theory of child raising, in addition to breaking out of the city, involved a running criticism bent on destroying every possible mask. If he felt you were being artificial, he said so, and in no uncertain terms. You were supposed to do the same, although I rarely did. A boy of ten cannot contend with a man.

"You're still better off than on a cruise ship" he said, once my wretching had stopped and he had followed it with some ginger ale. "Of course, you've never been on an ocean liner, have you, Cricket?"

"No."

"You're lucky. It's a form of imprisonment. In exchange for money, they assign you to a certain deck, serve you drinks, stuff you with food, and give you a shuffleboard stick to work it off with. Meanwhile all the interesting things on the boat are going on somewhere else: up in the pilothouse, back in the galley, down in the engine room, but you can't go there. Oh, no. Little chains are across all the key companionways to block your progress. But worst of all, you're incarcerated with a bunch of bloody Corinthians!"

"Yes," I gasped, not knowing what to say. Experience taught that when disagreed with, Harold would take as long as necessary to win you over. From my standpoint, his approach allowed no more room for self-expression than the supposed artificiality of my grandparents' life.

On this occasion he must have sensed some resistance, for he continued, "You don't agree that middleclass Americans are like blind, helpless larvae, Cricket? They're the very ones the worker ants carry up to the sunlight every morning to make them hatch, and down again to their cells at night. Helpless, helpless! A perfect example is the loss of your grandfather's yacht. One weekend he went down to the club for a cruise out among the San Juan Islands, and it was gone, stolen. I was older then and had played my football. I was willing to interrogate the club help, go from warehouse to warehouse, start throwing people around. But instead of accepting my advice and taking matters into his own hands, he refused to hire detectives or charter a plane or buy a gun just in case. All he did was notify the police, who had the gall to tell him that they could look for the criminals, but not the boat! I can't imagine how they expected to find the criminals without first finding the boat, but that was their story and he had to accept it, his lifestyle being what it was – back to work on Monday morning in that air-conditioned car with his manicured finger-nails on the steering wheel. That's what I call being a Corinthian!"

Harold's concept of getting back to the basics took a further turn the night we received a log through the bows. I was sound asleep when I felt the shock, followed by water welling up in my sleeping bag. The average child might have panicked, but my training had been thorough, and I nerved myself to wait for an appropriate moment to trade my bunk for his. Fortunately it came our first night off the ways. In replacing a plank, the shipwrights had found it necessary to use an extra piece of wood which now disturbed the place I usually put my pillow. After polishing it left and right and finding no comfort, I conceived a bright idea.

"This new board bothers my head, Harold," I said. "What is it called?"

"What!" I saw the anger flash through his face as he turned the wheel hard over. He was standing on the platform above the engine, and I knew he was having trouble. Normally his head would be stuck clear out into the night in order to see, but now he had to jerk it back every so often to keep from being doused. Sometimes I would hear the hiss of water on the stack and even the sound of my own heart as the engine stopped, which was the governor's response whenever the propeller came clear out of water.

"Wait!" Harold said, as the seas struck like a drum near my head, "that's a butt block!"

"What's a butt block?"

"God damn it! What do you think this is, the Easter Parade?" He cranked the wheel to miss what must have been an exceptionally high wave, for I felt myself go weightless. The stars came into the door, and then they seemed to withdraw like warriors on a crusade. That was what we were doing. Even at ten years of age I knew we weren't there to make a living. With his education he could have done that in a dozen ways. This was a vendetta!

"Now, what were you saying, Cricket? I'm sorry to speak so harshly, but in this weather you could easily knock the calking out of a floating coffin like this. All right, the purpose of a butt block is to join two planks. They're used to keep from turning the frames – what the Corinthians call ribs – into a pin cushion. What you're sleeping next to is really something to increase the structural integrity of the hull, so don't worry."

"Can I sleep in your bunk?"

"Go ahead, if you have to."

The problem was to get there. As oceans of

water swept past the windows and the whirling helm continued to cut him like a pie, I realized there was only one place I really wanted to be and that was back in Alaska. Sometimes the boat seemed to fly and even he stiffened as we bounced hard, two or three times, as though going down the steps of the Dexter Horton Building. What scared me most were those moments when even his eyes grew far away, as though this might be overkill.

Neah Bay is part of the Makah Indian Reservation, and while verging on the most dangerous waters in Puget Sound, it is also the most like Alaska. Instead of our evenings of conversation and cereal, which had proven much too risky, our habit now was to pause every morning before that familiar panorama of smoking cabins, swaying laundry, barking dogs, as we came in to deliver our fish. We were both homesick for that atmosphere of intimacy which our moments together could not duplicate. That required my mother's touch. I would usually have slept some during the night, and as soon as Harold collapsed in an effort to heal his fatigue, which often made him stagger like a drunk, I would head uptown. There was an Indian boy with whom I played the game of going to school. The fellow was totally illiterate, but I think our game helped to relieve the guilt I felt at missing classes. Harold's search for truth, it seemed, did not extend to making enough money to hire a regular deckhand. There was still another disadvantage of which his critical nature should have made him aware, had he been thinking. It is said that men must dream to retain their sanity, but with children there is a need to play, and with Harold you never could at all. The least flippancy would set him off.

One day I must have stayed away too long, for on returning to the boat, I found his bunk was empty. I was so scared I hid in the head. Shortly Harold returned and I began to relax as the familiar sounds went back and forth on deck, occasionally nearing me as he came into the cabin, but never for long. One of the things you learn on a boat is to develop a sense of sound almost like a blind man's. Therefore, I soon noticed that some strange noises were taking place out on deck – an opening of the hatch covers, which was unusual since we'd already washed down after delivering our fish. I didn't see what Harold could possibly be wanting in there, but I didn't move. The seat gripped my buttocks like the mouth of a well. Finally he began to shout.

"Cricket! Where are you? Answer, for God's sake! I can't go back to Alaska without you. I could never face your mother. Come on, if you care for me at all!"

Such 'heart on the sleeve' pronouncements were by now too common to move me much. If nothing else, two months with him had taught me the value of artificiality wherever I found it. Instead of giving in, I climbed up on the seat to get a better view. His ankle was there outside the porthole, but vanished almost immediately, to be followed by fluttering noises whose source I couldn't quite see. It sounded like flags were being lowered, and then there was silence, which I found less agreeable, especially when I remembered how the anemones looked far down on the creosote pilings. They floated about like human hair.

It suddenly came to me he was going overboard,

14

and before this could happen, opening me to a lifetime of ridicule about the Little Lord Fauntleroy who sat indifferently on the toilet while his father dove to save his life, I hurried out on deck. I knew it would be bad, but the expression on Harold's face was like nothing I'd ever seen before. In fact, I barely recognized him. He wore a supercilious sneer which I'd only seen in family albums, but was so basic to those snapshots, now that I think of it, that it challenged the famous Hapsburg lip. And it was then – I think the only time during my childhood – that I grasped what it was he was fighting and why he went to Alaska and even what it was to be a Corinthian.

Bride of the Fleet

Dear Diedre,

Fishing is not going well. We've moved our string a half dozen times in the last two weeks, and all we get are tanner crab. Too bad there's no market for them. I'll let you know right away if our luck changes. Meanwhile I think we'll have to postpone the wedding.

The truth was his doubts went much deeper, and knowing this, he added: I feel farther away from you than ever up here on the Alaskan fishing grounds. I'll be sending you portions of my journal regularly.

The first thing we saw today on rounding Point Naskowhak was Park's schooner, the *Solar System*. It was too big to go inside the small boat harbor and had to be moored outside against the ferry dock. As we danced forward through the light chop that was scalloping the breakwater, the rock-like solidity of this vessel made our own feel like a dory. The *Solar System*'s ironbark guards resembled the banding on a sea chest, and more water spilled from its live tanks in a few minutes than we could easily have pumped in an hour. Whatever crab Heinie and I catch are delivered dry.

"Lucky for you he's here," said Heinie. "When Park goes out he stays until he gets a load. He's a greedy bastard."

"I know," I said, "but we've got to change our luck. I'm sure he'll help us."

"Him?" The skipper pointed ahead to a wreck that was so heavily covered with moss and barnacles it might have been a fallen tree. "The reason the Coast Guard took so long to find his first boat was he won't even tell his own wife where he goes!"

Together Heinie and I set out for Park's luxury home on the Slough. Seldovia is built on the face of a cliff, and the only way you can get around is by boardwalk. Now it stretched ahead of us like a window washer's scaffolding, handrails in poor repair, planks slippery with moss. Growing out from the hillside were big elephant-eared vines that got in our way, and in places it was all a man could do to get by. Through the rich fall foliage we moved like boxers sparring against invisible opponents. That pretty well describes our current relationship. With the steady decline in our catch, the skipper seems to disagree with me just on principle. I've been trying to get him to try new grounds all season, but it's not until the equinoctial storms that he'll even consider it!

"Let's get a move on," he said, as we passed the wreck. Its naked frames were like the bones of a whale, yet its engine appeared no bigger than a human heart. Until signing on as a deckhand, I hadn't realized the devastating nature of a too-close human relationship. With all the comings and goings in the city, you just never arrive at the point I've reached with Heinie.

Finally he stopped and raised an arm. I looked up and high in the trees were some picture windows offering a pretty reflection of the Slough in the dying light. After all the subtle pressure I've been applying to get us out of this backwater – a woman's wiles, if you'll pardon the expression – it

Bride of the Fleet

was a relief to see him move up the steps and into a narrow doorway, where he knocked on the first wood that stopped him.

In a moment a woman appeared, bringing with her a faint odor of polished wood. It seemed to match the deepening colors that came from the picture windows at the far end of the hall.

"Is Stormy in?" Heinie asked, using the name our lesser brothers in the fleet have applied to the only man I know who's making money at crab fishing.

The woman stiffened. "My husband, Park Wendt, is."

Heinie patted that belly which I see slopping grossly onto the galley table at every meal, and spoke as though he relished his words.

"We'll see him before he goes to bed, then."

"May I ask what for?"

"I want Park to tell this kid that if we leave the estuary, I'll be paying widows' compensation just like him. Maybe you didn't know. He's planning to get married!"

The woman smiled in bafflement and I shook

20

my head, hoping she would see what I'd been going through. As a skipper's wife, she ought to be able to understand. One of the things I've learned this summer is that being a deckhand is the nearest thing to being a wife. The pressures that build during round-the-clock exposure to another person are almost unbelievable.

"Are you sure this can't wait till morning?" she said. "He just got in."

Heinie plowed right on. "Wait? No, ma'am. Haven't you heard? *Cancer magister* is already making for deep water. That's Latin. *Cancer* means crab and *magister* means king – like yes, your majesty; no, your majesty. We may look like ignorant fishermen, but we're educated, by golly!"

As she left, Heinie was sawing the air like one of those nightbirds that wakes in confusion on the water when hit by the decklights.

In a minute a large man with wiry black hair appeared in the woman's place. I expected him to be out of sorts, but instead he merely looked interested, watchful. What a relief! Right away I sensed an interior capacity to understand, which is what my skipper chiefly lacks. Park appeared as a man of discernment right down to his new woolen socks, which were white and fluffy in a way that washing never gives. He's supposed to be a greedy man, a spender of human lives in his mad quest for crab, but that was not my sense; and believe me, after a season on a boat you know these things. Asking us to step in, he first cautioned me about the uncarpeted floor, which was slick as a laundry chute. He even took my arm. I have to admit it was a little tricky walking in my dirty socks over that slippery surface with nothing to hold onto, not even curtains.

"You'll have to excuse the state of the house," he said, as we entered the main room, "but my wife has been redecorating."

Some explanation did seem necessary, for the room was bare as a gymnasium.

"Does she paint?" I asked, finding unspeakable relief in using such words. The further I get from that tiny fo'c's'le where I live with the fat skipper, the more I remember the man I was, the one who adored you and whom you loved. It's all so difficult up here. It's reached the point where we even argue over who washes the dishes and who dries.

"No, as a matter of fact, she makes pillows," said Park. "She feels that bare floors show them off better. What do you think?"

I picked up one of the cushions and was surprised to find it had arms and legs.

"My fiancée works in stitchery too," I said. "I think the three-dimensional effects are better than what you find in painting."

"Well, what can I do for you fellows?" Although still courteous, Park had finished with the tour. I also noticed that he was addressing Heinie now, instead of me. To that extent he was still a skipper. What arcane customs fishing has! We pass other boats in the fleet and the captains talk as though the men on deck don't even exist. At the dock Heinie is off and away before our slab is properly tied to the pilings, and I don't know when he's coming back until I see him, maybe an hour, maybe a weekend. It's hard to be a deckhand, and in this improved setting the artificiality of the difference struck me even more. In our dress was a similarity that marked us all as fishermen: the heavy woolen trousers held up by suspenders, a snowline on the forehead visible now in the absence of a knit cap, the shirtsleeves shortened so as to avoid the chafing of wet cuffs, which is one of the most annoying things about deck work. The least humanity would make the inconveniences of our trade quite bearable, but Heinie is a living argument for equal rights.

"The kid's going to kill us both," he said, "unless you can put some sense in his head. Where you fish, how long would it take the sand fleas to strip the meat from a human body?"

Park looked thoughtful. "Oh, I would say about three hours."

"But a small boat could save its crab, couldn't it?" I asked. "There must be some way to keep our crab alive on the open inlet."

"Better ask him first how to save your neck in the hundred knot winds." Heinie sent a pillow tipping and turning across the floor, its arms reaching in all directions like a man clutching at straws. "It can be flat calm one minute and blowing a gale the next."

Park looked after the manikin, but said nothing. As if sensing a question that could not be resolved in a minute, he raised a hand. "Say, how would you fellows like a drink? I've been out for two straight weeks and am a little dry."

Graciously indicating that we could make ourselves comfortable, Park padded off for the kitchen. The yellow glow under the bedroom door was instantly eclipsed by the explosion of light at the sink, where our host appeared, his kinky hair like the proverbial black sheep's. It took Park only a minute to mix the drinks and then he was back. Apart from being in his stocking feet, his stride was firm and gave no sign that he was ready for bed. In fact, now that he had found friendly ears, he seemed perfectly willing to make a night of it.

"We really went over the top this year," he said, stretching out again on the oiled floor. He brought some pillows near him and seemed indifferent to the sweat-like stains our glasses were causing on their ornate surfaces. "One of the most interesting things we did was to make a film for fishermen in South America. They have this little crab called a centolla, and on the last day of our trip the educational people from Anchorage flew a special crew out to shoot us. We've developed a few new techniques, you know: tilted entrances, a trap that collapses, the hydraulic pot launcher."

I was momentarily confused. "But how did they land?"

The obviousness of my question stopped Park only a moment. "It was a helicopter and we have a big foredeck."

"Oh, it might be a little hairy," said Heinie, "but I guess we could chance it. Our boat is barely thirty feet and we could scoot up a tree at night like a spruce chicken or maybe get in behind the falls at Akjemguiga."

Now Park laughed out loud for the first time. Like any outsider, he had been trying to avoid what looked like a family quarrel. Having acquired the right to comment on account of the scene we'd made in his house, he took this opportunity to set the record straight for both of us.

"You know, this business about uncharted waters is just a big story. Everywhere the sea is the same, wet and blue. Well, isn't it? They may suspend your insurance for going off the edge of the map, but that's because they've never been there themselves." Now he closed his eyes. "There are worse things than blank spots on a chart, believe me."

It was at this point that his wife appeared. She was dressed in a bathrobe and her hair was down over her back in thick waves that reminded me of the flow from the *Solar System's* scuppers. None of us moved. She was obviously ready for bed and ready for Park to come to her, but he remained poised like an orator waiting for the passage of an interruption.

"Is there anything I can do for you, dear?" he said, at last.

"Please get off the pillows. They weren't meant for that." Then she disappeared as I have done when the fat skipper wouldn't move and the only hope was to arouse his curiosity.

"We're not hurting them none, are we?" said Heinie, as soon as her door closed.

"Why don't you boys go in the kitchen and fix yourselves another drink," said Park. With an uncharacteristic lack of dignity he was struggling to get to his feet, but like a dog on glare ice, getting nowhere fast. "I'll be right back."

"I've got to go back and check the lines," I said, wrenching myself up against the wall. There was no danger to our little boat here inside the harbor, but I said I'd write.

For the first time this year there comes a sense of hopelessness – for us, for everybody. Until now, I'd thought that love could conquer all, but I'm beginning to doubt it. In view of what I've seen today, I can easily believe the wreck on the beach was caused by the perverse reaction of two people, one to the other. The rage against such Siamese relationships is everywhere you look. At least you've got to admit that something is very wrong when a man will prefer a little money, the false notoriety of television coverage, to a lovely wife; for that is what our hostess was. I wouldn't, but then I don't know what I'd do. I'm only human. I can only explain their problem in terms of what I've been experiencing, and that is that the effect of imprisoning two people together turns them into monsters. For weeks on end Park hides himself in uncharted waters, and when he does come home it is to sit around with his friends, crushing those very pillows into which his wife has sewn all her passions.

Hoping to hear from you soon,

P.W.

The Compleat Moose Hunter

Now we're going to have a little discussion about moose hunting. You can carry a gun in your truck and shoot one on the highway going to and from work, or you can spot one with a plane. All you have to remember if you use a plane is not to shoot it on the same day you see it. Some folks think that might be hard to enforce, but it isn't. The protection agent simply removes his glove and feels the engine. If the cowling is warm, you're guilty. If cold, innocent. It's about as easy as getting thrown out of school for insufficient interest. I humbly hope this paper will get me back in the eleventh grade.

Another way to get a moose is out of season. This is ideal for homesteaders, because unless you have a light plant there's no way to hold your meat. The regular season ends in September, and after that it takes about two months for the weather to get cold enough so the meat won't rot. In Alaska there has always been a subsistence law for trappers and explorers which allows them to kill game any time of year, but everyone supposes a homesteader has his own food. They're crazy! Up here no one farms without a government subsidy. We're hard up. You see pictures of cabbages so big they won't fit in a wheelbarrow and strawberries the size of ox hearts, but growing them is just a stunt. It would take a 100-K to set up right to farm, and if Mom and me had a 100-K, we wouldn't be farming. We'd be living it up in Palm Beach, Florida!

Boy, it's hard to think when you're hungry. As I lie here on this couch Mom made out of an old truck seat, my belly rumbles. It's all we have left from our trip up the Highway after Pop died. A chewed pencil is no substitute for a thick moosemeat sandwich dripping with mayonnaise and horse radish and catsup and mustard. At the thought of soft backstrap which smells so much like the hunting grounds up around Slackwater I could go there blindfolded, my teeth bite down on nothing. Animals smell of what they eat. I once shot a ptarmigan in a field of wild strawberries, and it tasted like fruit with feathers. This is good writing, isn't it?

You know, I could get good grades if I wanted to, but it's a little dangerous. My friend Rex, who was just sixteen, could write like a professional, but what did it get him? Mrs. Schimmerhorn accused him of plagiarism, and he was so shook up he committed suicide. That was too bad. Just before it happened, she tried to apologize, but by then it was too late. His skin was all broken out and some of us thought he had syphilis. One of its symptoms is pimples, isn't it? Mr. Felt said it was the time of life, but I don't know whether he meant Rex's or Mrs. Schimmerhorn's. I like Mr. Felt. He was the one who fixed it up so I could get back in school by writing 3,000 words. He said we should all try to understand Mrs. Schimmerhorn, explaining that in my case it had somehow become a personal thing, although I don't know how. He was right when he said some people are sleeping when they should be thinking, and vice versa.

But let's get back to the subject. For openers, shooting a moose requires the right gun. Even killing a deer is harder than you think. Before Pop died we lived on a big farm in Musselshell County in Montana. Mom came to Alaska to better herself, along with the Fifty-Niners, but I don't think serving drinks in a bar is very good, do you? On the farm we had this big green field and early in the morning before anyone was up I used to sit in my bedroom window, watching for deer. The grass was a different color with the dew on it, a kind of silver, but it would turn black wherever you stepped. One time I pumped a whole box of .22 ammo into a young fork'n horn, but it wouldn't go down. When I ran out to see what was wrong, it was almost tame. You could walk right up to it, but it wouldn't let you kill it, not quite. It was sort of like me and teachers.

The end of the story is the deer got away. I chased it all over the farm, trying to club it with my rifle, stab it, beat it with rocks. Finally I broke the stock of my rifle over its head, but it just kept going. Pop found it the next spring a few feet from where I quit, just a pile of fur and dirty bones. That was a shame, but I guess we all end up that way sooner or later.

How am I doing? I sure would like some of that

whipped squash they serve in the cafeteria. At the moment all we have in the house are some old rotten potatoes, and they stink to beat the band! We don't have a root cellar yet and first they froze and then they got warm and spoiled. Mrs. Schimmer-horn says all the great poets did their best work when they were hungry, but I'm not so sure about that. This business of eating only when Mom comes home with a fistful of money makes my head spin.

Well, what else is new? I think we should go out and get us a moose right now. Of course, it's illegal, but you've forgotten. I have a poetic license! We'll use my Mauser. You can tell it's an old war gun because there are little birds on the barrel. These are German eagles, but they're not there for decoration. They're proof marks. There is also a number which Pop used to say we should send in to a hunting magazine sometime. Some battlefield trophies are not safe to shoot. When the Germans started losing, they began making guns out of any old thing – church bells, engine blocks, sewing machines. In writing this paper I could easily end up picking the steel out of my teeth. How's that for interest?

Meanwhile back at the ranch . . . I should say

garbage dump which the bulldozer accidentally made when it cleared our field. The hole is supposed to be covered, but we haven't done that yet. Why spoil the view? You can see magpies out there right now. "Pies," Mrs. Schimmerhorn calls them, but they don't look very edible to me. If you want the truth, they're loud, stringy, repulsive birds whose white and black feathers make them resemble underfed penguins. Even more aggressive are the camp robbers. Greenhorns sometimes mistake these birds for squirrels because of their purplish plumage, which looks like fur. There are not many squirrels. Mom says they ate the insulation out of our roof and died. This has been a bad winter.

Okay, so you're wondering where this moose is going to come from when you can't tame or breed them legally. Watch as I pound the butt of the gun against a tree. The bulls think that some other male is challenging them. I guess they're pretty much like people, except that people have souls. I bet you can't guess who this one reminds me of. Right now our moose is showing its head, just the tips of its ears and its eyes. You can't tell what sex it is, but who cares? When you shoot out of season, they're all antlerless anyway. It must feel us coming because its head starts going up and down like a balloon, that big eye watching just like Mrs. Schimmerhorn's on the day I got kicked out of school for offering her a chocolate-coated turd.

Now that you're really hooked on my paper, let's stop to consider the moose diet. I've been counting the words and I need more. They eat birch, cottonwood, and alder in that order, mainly the buds. It's not hard to tell when a moose has been in your field because its teeth cut sharply at an angle. It looks like shears. Fooled me the first year, though. I went out in spring after the snow melted and at first I thought some bad-ass had gone around topping all our saplings. I may be dumb, but out in the woods the simplest problem can be quite difficult. For instance, what would you do if a moose started sticking out its tongue and knocking its knees together? [1]

Now don't get excited. We're not going to kill

---

[1] Hint: that means it's getting ready to charge.

anything yet. First you've got to study all the background material so that when you do finally pull the trigger, you won't care. "If the road ahead is not clear," Pop used to say, "just get down and piss." Take tracking, for instance. The hunter is not supposed to walk right in the animal's footsteps. That's because wild animals have a sixth sense that tells them when they're being followed. The correct way to track is to go forward in long loops, picking up the trail from time to time, but that takes practice. Okay, I'm not going to keep you after school for that. I've spent enough time watching tired teachers correcting papers to spare you that sight. It can be disillusioning, like catching one smoking out behind the outhouse.

Here, why don't you hold the gun? It will be a good experience to learn to kill on command. Mr. Felt, our school psychologist, says my problem is I've somehow avoided the socializing process, but I'm trying. There, rest it in the fork of that tree and start working the hillside. It's like in a war. You can see puffs of snow and bits of bark where the slugs hit, and you're only missing by an acre or two.

Fortunately, it can't think. That's your big advantage and never forget it. Even I feel like I've been too thoughtless lately. Don't act on impulse – stalk like I've been saying. You'll get along better and people will respect you.

I hate to sound like I've developed interest so quickly, but I have. The system works. Congratulations! You've just bagged your first moose. We'll enter it in that supersecret file they keep locked in the office. So you won't lose your breakfast, I'll go forward and cut its throat for you. Not everyone is like our gym teacher, who was supposed to have packed a thousand pound bull home on his back. He'd forgotten to cut it up and it froze, but that was the least of his worries. When he came into town with its legs stuck straight up like horns, everyone started blazing away, including the principal from his office window. He's always telling us, "Obey the rules. It doesn't matter if they're right or wrong. It's what you have to do if you want to join the adult community." I guess he was a philosophy major in college or something, but I entirely agree. From where I sit that school lunch looks pretty good.

Old Man Winter

The look of the sea had changed. It was like a crystal spring poisoned with cyanide. Instead of old snow patches the color of tobacco juice, there was a gentle smattering of white on the surrounding hills, like pollen. Almost overnight the shoreline had become a graveyard of falling leaves and broken branches above which ravens made lone sentinel flights, their voices croaking loudly when anything moved below. To be in the open now was to be out of place, an opinion generally shared by my crewmen. Although the fall chum salmon were still running, they wanted to quit.

"All right," I said, one morning when all they would do was complain, "you may think you've seen the last of this net, but you haven't. No one is getting paid until every broken mesh is mended!"

The trip to port was much less jubilant than

usual, but back at the cannery I made arrangements with the watchman to stretch the net out in the loft, where at least they'd be protected from the weather. Like my deckhands, the watchman wasn't keen on our doing gear work now. It would mean having to run the big generator to provide lights, but considering our long season of consistent production, he could hardly refuse.

That night a strange thing happened. When we went down to move the boat, which was necessary to prevent it from banging against the pilings and keeping us awake, the gears wouldn't mesh. Someone said it was divine retribution, but I knew better than that. It didn't take me long to figure out that the clutch on the marine gear had given out. Actually, I told them, it was good luck to break down here at the dock instead of out at sea next spring, which surely would have happened if we'd quit with the others. Accommodating both jobs would require only a slight change of plans. I would have to get someone else to direct the hanging of the net, which I had gone so far as to strip from the lines, while I tore into the engine.

"Who around here knows how to hang a seine?" I asked the watchman.

At the sound of my words his cheeks grew large and he blew out lengthily. "You're not stuck, I hope."

"Now don't start giving me that. I've got some mechanical problems, that's all."

He showed some relief, but still looked skeptical. "Well, there was Handsome, but he's usually hard to raise once he goes back to the Village."

"I'll get him. I'll call him on the radio right now."

The watchman shrugged the shoulders of his old blue overalls. "You can do whatever you want. Just remember, hanging gear in the fall is like Fourth of July in February. You can do it, but a lot of fishermen I know would rather whittle a plug for their ass and take the first tide south. Good luck."

It wasn't hard to raise the Village, for with fishing over, there was nothing much to do but drink and talk, and the CB chatter never ceased. The radio operator even sounded glad to co-operate. In fact he promised he would! Winter might be coming on, but it wasn't as far advanced as some around here said. The web man would be delivered that very day.

"Good riddance!" said the fellow who brought the man called Handsome over in a skiff. I saw what looked like a bundle being pushed up and over the bows. When it hit the water, it made a splash. A moment later something rose to its feet. It was a man.

"Hey, where's the web man?" I yelled. It was one thing to be running a nursery school for spoiled deckhands and another to play Alcoholics Anonymous.

The skiff man must have heard my voice, for he slowed his engine. "If he tells you he can't work because his people have quit, don't believe him. He doesn't have any!"

Then he swung the boat in a sharp circle, catching the new arrival's feet with a wave just as Handsome left the water. The next moment the skiff was moving at full throttle out across the bay, the bottom flapping like the sole of an old shoe. I turned my attention to my new employee. He was limping up the beach, and now I wasn't sure whether he was drunk or merely old. Like many beaches adjacent to processing plants in Alaska, this one was a mixture of mud and kelp and clams and old rusty machinery.

"Is he going to be all right?" I asked the watchman, who had come down to see what all the noise was about. During this time the web man had never once looked my way, but at the very last he had taken hold of the watchman's arm and they seemed to be talking.

"I think so," said the watchman, "but before Handsome can work he says he's going to need some underwear, also some cigarettes."

"Well, let's get him some from the store!"

The watchman grimaced as though I still hadn't gotten the point. "Haven't I told you, everything is shut for the winter? I'll tell you what I'll do, though, just to get you out of my hair. I'll loan Handsome some of my own underwear, and maybe one of your men will have some extra smokes."

That day there was no complaining, but neither was there joy. It was too serious. With the winter storms due to start at any time, the pieces of the net could theoretically be bagged, but the boat couldn't. Out at the dock face, where it lay dead in the water, it would make an easy target for the first north-easter. Unless we got it going before the weather changed, it could easily be broken to pieces against the pilings.

I decided it would be making the best use of my time if I got things going first in the loft and then went directly to work on the engine. From experience I knew that web work was boring, which was one of the reasons I'd imposed it, also why I was glad of the extra man, both for his company and his expertise. When men are working on a net, there are certain distinctive sounds – the rattle of corks on their lines or the hiss of web as it's pulled across the floor – that create the same sense of community that chirping birds do in a tree. In fact, it was the loss of Handsome's "voice" that first alerted me to the fact he wasn't working.

"Say, what's going on here?" I said, locating him at a back window, where he was smoking a cigarette and looking out at the passing clouds. "In a minute I'll be going down to work on the reduction gear, and they need you to help square off."

Without haste the web man turned and smiled with child-like innocence. "I'm resting my eyes. A doctor once told me it was important to change the distances. Otherwise I might go blind."

"Well, you're not going to go blind in this short time, Handsome. Also the lights are on." I looked back just in time to catch the eye of the hand who'd given him the cigarettes. He was so angry that in setting a knot he accidentally snapped his twine. I knew what I had to do, and fast.

"Come on, man, we're fighting to save the boat, don't you understand? These guys are eager, but it takes someone with your experience to spot the web along the lines. Let's go now, we're losing time."

"Oh, and another thing," said Handsome, in that same syrupy tone. "During the summer they have mug-up at ten, three, and nine at night, and my stomach bothers me unless I have something on it. I'd really like some pastries."

I went down to the boat and turned up the stove, preparatory to opening a box of cake mix. Then, in order not to be guilty of involuntary manslaughter, I pulled up the hatch in the floor and crawled down in the bilge. It was cold down there and smelled of old fish. There, with a droplight banging me in the forehead, I forced myself to do a job that was ten times harder than what the others were doing, which didn't mean it was impossible. You simply grabbed a wrench and went at the rusted bolts one at a time. Winter! Were we men or animals of instinct?

I couldn't tell what time it was. My cake was long since done. Where I worked, there was only a twelve-volt bulb, but it must have been late afternoon when a shadow warned me someone had come into the cabin. I was expecting the worst and was relieved when the watchman's face appeared above me like a bucket at the top of a well.

"Well, how are you doing?" he said, squinting his eyes down to where I sat Indian-style.

"Not bad. I haven't sheared any bolts yet."

"I see you burned your cake."

"Yeah, it's easy to do when you're as cold as I am. Say, what's with this Handsome, anyway? I thought he was supposed to be a web man!"

"He is a web man, but you're working him at the

wrong time of year." The watchman paused and I
thought I caught the giratory motion of an animal
winding the breeze for danger. Then the head and
shoulders centered themselves once more in the
aperture above me. "Don't get me wrong. In the
summer he works slick as soap with someone
watching over him, but this is winter and he's a little
ornery. Just don't get him mad."

I decided it was time to warm my body and
hoisted myself up to where the world looked
familiar again. Through the galley windows I was
glad to see that nothing basic had changed. The
cannery roof still had the same hard line, less, of
course, its summer gulls. Above and behind were
the identical slopes which had been logged to
provide pulp for export, but whose stumps now
had the look of tombstones. Joining the sky were
the gullied heights where nothing moved but
boulders, and soon not even those. All would be
frozen solid.

"Mind if I try a piece?" asked the watchman,
choosing one of the knives that lay in the sink. For a
long time now my crewmen had shirked the dishes.

"Sure, anything to keep the population happy. I know men have to eat to work, but it's another thing to run around keeping them in diapers, don't you think?"

The watchman paused with the cake knife, his tongue on one of his molars. "Be careful now. If it's Handsome you're talking about, he's stronger than either of us."

"That piece of human wreckage?" I took a seat by the stove and shoved my hands inside. You had to be careful, for when the skin lost all feeling, you could easily burn yourself. "The way it looks to me, he's already drunk up half his season's earnings."

"That's true." The watchman was chewing noisily, his false teeth popping. "But if you measure a man's strength by his willingness to suffer, then Handsome could whip the living daylights out of either one of us. He already has over at the Village."

I didn't answer. This was winter talk. Even more than the cold in the bilge, I hated its stultification of everything real and was determined to resist it.

As if unaware of my mood, the watchman prattled on to the galley in general. "One time Handsome was giving a party at a friend's house. It was in December or January, I don't remember which, and after trying every way he knew to break it up, Hans Holm – that's the man you saw in the skiff today – had a bright idea. He turned off all the heat, opened the doors and windows, and left his namesake and his buddies to make up their own minds. The plan worked perfectly, except that when Hans returned home in the morning, there was an odd smell in the yard. It looked as though the snow had been urinated on, only it wasn't urine, it was a whole winter's stove oil. They'd chopped the barrels!"

The watchman raised the cake knife hopefully, and I nodded for him to go ahead. This was better than I thought. If he kept this up, I'd soon be fearing for my boat!

"Thanks. Take last winter now. Handsome was living on welfare. They sell no liquor there in the Village, so he was flying into town to make his purchases. It's an odd thing, but a welfare check is just big enough for one round-trip ticket by air and a gallon of port. You wonder why we're paying taxes. Anyway, Hans finally had enough of it."

"So he put him out in the snow."

"How did you guess?" For the first time since our arrival at the cannery the watchman looked genuinely impressed.

"Don't let it bother you. It came to me when I was sitting down in the bilge. Please go on."

But I'd broken his stride. Instead of eating, the watchman was staring through the hole in the floor where the droplight was swinging to and fro. It all seemed far away now, even to me. Some greasy bolts sat in a metal can that was wedged against a floor timber. The bell housing of the engine resembled an iron lung from which a patient has just been snatched. I knew it would take a supreme effort to go back down there, no matter what my theories. Finally he shook his head.

"I guess Handsome sat outside the house a good long while. In fact, it wasn't until he was ready to die that Hans would even look at him." The watchman licked his fingers contemplatively, as though trying to visualize the scene exactly as it was. It was obviously an incident to which he'd given much thought.

"People said in the end Handsome just lay there

like a husky, all covered with snow. The only sign of life was the hole where his breath came out, and right at the end Hans was running out of the house every five minutes to see if it was still there."

I waited, but he seemed to have finished. "And you say that makes him stronger, a lush outlasting a friend who's the only one who cares whether he lives or dies?"

"You bet!" The watchman flexed his jaw muscles truculently. "You achievers are all the same. You're just weaklings. Take what you're doing here. If you weren't afraid your boat would sink, you'd leave it to the elements like the rest of the people around here do. A child can save a boat, but it takes a man to build one. I've been watching you, and every move you make is a way of avoiding pain. You're afraid of being outfished, so you fish like hell, but what does it prove? Worry makes you rich and pretty soon people begin to think you're a bigshot, when it's really just the opposite. Compared to the Handsomes of the world, it's pure cowardice!"

"Say, would you mind taking this up to the

boys?" I put the cake in his hands so hard it made him jump. I was really getting enough of this.

"Aye, aye, sir, anything to help." The watchman started toward the door. "The last thing I want is to have you hanging around here all winter. It can be a pretty nice time of year."

Whitemare

At ground level the ice appeared like the sides of a quarry. Even the plane reacted as if trapped, running the wobbly course of a downed insect the moment it touched. I had been afraid that in case of an early spring someone might jump my fishing sites, but now I saw I had forgotten the size of the shelf ice. A moment ago it had appeared as a porcelain frame holding the carefully fitted glass of the entire inlet. Until it melted, a fisherman would have to jump or climb, as though off the roof of a building, every time he went near the water. The sky was lighter than when I had left, but with so much snow in the woods I doubted that anyone would have been out setting buoys.

The steps let down and the plane shook as I came out on the ramp. I had a woolen suit on, but the air seived through it. Through that same inner eye that had been seeing the first buds of spring I could visualize the window-screen weave of the fabric. At the same time, I sensed that I, the well-dressed traveler, was like a piece of carry-on luggage, something I better not lose sight of. The drawn curtain of the trees was real!

"You could have waited a month and still been early," said a fisherman who was waiting at the bottom. During the winter I wrote him letters in the hope he would be flattered enough to meet me. It was good to see him. Where I'd failed was in believing this correspondence would keep me in touch. A scarf lifted his chin like a stock. His many layers of clothing made him resemble an inflated diving suit.

"You must be right, Adrian. I don't see too many planes on floats around here yet."

"Well, it's just as well." He stopped me from falling on the last step. "You must have seen the buoys."

"No! What buoys?"

"On your sites! I think somebody's jumped your locations."

Before we could go into it, my bags were tossed

out and I had to snatch them quickly before they
sank through to water, which was percolating up
everywhere. Although the woods were still a cata-
combs of shadows choked deep in snow, places that
had been cleared were breaking up in the sun. The
country was in transition, and I had the feeling that I
was too. By going away I had dulled my animal
instinct. It was a little frightening.

As soon as we had everything, we made for the
parking lot. I noticed that everywhere I looked the
sun caromed back and forth, creating a glare that
made it difficult to see where you were going, even
among the cars. I had to concentrate, once or twice
touching Adrian's heavy woolen sleeve, to keep
from going in over my shoes.

"You seem to have wintered well," he said,
when we had placed my bags in the car, which he
did three at a time.

"It's nice getting away, but good to be back." I
would have said more, but since he had been here
all winter, it would have been unkind. I knew he
had been thinking of me all winter in a certain way,
as calloused and dirty — my chief claim on him —

whereas I had been visiting museums. At one point, shortly after leaving teaching, I had tried to immerse myself in this cold and emptiness fulltime, but the northern culture was just too raw. Summer was bad enough, but men grew increasingly illogical as winter turned abstract. Maybe there wasn't much relation between the exhibits I'd recently seen at the Smithsonian and the actual history – Lindberg's plane and crossing the Atlantic – but at least the Washington galleries were clean and well-ordered. Their psychological effect was positive. You could walk through the tunnel under the Capitol and not even think of blowing it up. Once more I was back in the conflict. What was it Service said, "Fierce to defy and defend"?

"Sure you don't have anything else?" Adrian was trying to rock the car out of the frozen ruts his tires had made during the short time he had been waiting. I had placed a lumpy satchel between us, and he was having trouble shifting.

"Just books, Adrian." I pulled them nearer me. They were the antidote I would need when this whole place became too oppressive. It always did, even with the practical work of fishing. "What's this about the buoys?"

As though suddenly recalled to what we had been talking about, he slowed the car in the wild career homesteaders use to cross an exceptionally slick surface. We bumped out on the highway.

"I would have written, but had a problem with my well. I hit hardpan!"

"It's okay. What could you have done?" This ice I saw on both sides of us, holding chunks of debris like jujubes, hadn't left much room for maneuver. My fishing locations could have gone under and no one would really have been the wiser until they came up again in spring. Faced by the sheer grandeur of the paralysis, I was feeling a little easier. The astronauts might have gained the moon, but here you did well to reach your outhouse. Any fishing activity seemed highly unlikely.

I would have passed it off as rumor, except these stories always had some basis in fact. I'd lived here and done my share of gossiping. After the Good Friday quake I'd helped embroider the story of a man who could no longer walk upright, but had to move with the support of the walls, as though the ground were still swaying. Another had to do with a principal who was fired for touching a girl's private parts while robing her for the outdoors. A hunting accident gave rise to a tale about a bear that had eaten a man in the presence of his family. Asylums of the world arise! To live here in winter was to take a special excursion down through a Plutonian world of frozen filth and mental aberration. I might have known that by the time my bags were claimed, I would be in the midst of another blazing scandal. I simply hadn't expected to be the target.

"I don't suppose anyone snowshoed out to see," I said.

"Not me!" Adrian's voice expressed shock that I would even ask. "I make it a rule never to mess with a place that's been broke into. I might get blamed!"

I could see him looking at me from the corners of his eyes to see if I believed. I looked straight ahead. There was nothing you could do when people insisted on being yokels. I wanted to say that in more civilized places your worst enemy would do more, but it wouldn't have done any good. I'd had my reward by going Outside, and now I had to "pay the bill," as Service said. I just couldn't understand why I hadn't seen the buoys. In my search for telltale signs of spring I'd been switching from one side of the plane to the other ever since we left Anchorage.

I studied the familiar landscape, perversely draped in white like summer chairs. Across its back the cleared highway speared into the woods like an unlit cigar. Although maintained, the road was still full of frost and in many places the surface had developed cracks like a glacier. As we rode along, whole pieces would subside together, making a muffled sound like lead. The clipping trees gave me the feeling of the last broken frames before the start of a film. It would be good. If what Adrian said were true, I'd have to use physical force to re-establish myself, and precisely because of my recent proximity to civilization, I would be at a disadvantage. As though speaking of just another inconvenience of winter, he said, "Juice is back."

"Juice! I thought he was in jail!"

"No, after knifing that boy for taking his seat at

the restaurant, Juice took off. The marshal's shiplap shack wouldn't hold him. It wouldn't even hold a nice guy like you." He gave me a condescending smile I hadn't seen in a long while. I knew it would become more commonplace as the summer wore on. To avoid just this sort of assault, more than because I believed him, I directed his attention back to the story.

"What did Juice do after he stabbed the boy?"

"Well, for a while he was back at his shop, working on an old Caterpillar for a neighbor. When the neighbor wouldn't pay, Juice had to clobber the tractor."

I went bolt upright, hitting my head thanks to an unusually nasty bump.

"How does he get away with that stuff? That man is a killer!"

"Not a killer, a homesteader." Adrian was showing further signs of impatience. I knew I'd have to be careful. Public opinion in these parts was like the product of a religious conclave and you didn't tamper with it. He looked at me meaningfully, indicating that if I would just be patient he'd tell me the rest.

"He shot the tractor, set it afire, and filled all the cylinders with cement."

"Now I've heard everything!" I turned away, trying to lose myself in the landscape out the window, but the view was temporarily obscured by the road sander, which was passing near our doors. There was the hammering of a Gatling gun as we took the gravel broadside.

Adrian sighed. "Nothing lasts in this country."

"No." I let my feet down in the tire chains. It was always a relief when you gave your linen and shoe leather up for lost and just got down in the dirt and rolled with the rest of them, only today it was starting sooner than usual. There was no question that my fishing shack would make an excellent hideout, hidden as it was between a hundred-foot mud bluff and, at this time of year, a fifteen-foot wall of ice. I was rested, I knew how the world was, but in spite of that I felt my sanity tottering. I was sure now Adrian's scruples had not prevented him from following up the rumor. He'd been remembering Juice's reputation for crotching men in the ribs when they were down on barroom floors. These people were above all practical, refusing to be trapped by fine feelings. It was too bad because I always wanted this country on my own terms, wishing against reason that life here could be lived at a civilized minimum.

As we approached the area where the suspect lived, I tried to tell myself it was too soon. The fish hadn't even come yet. When they did, all would be well. The sinister odor I smelled rose only from the rotting vegetation slain by the cold. All the lesser plants had frozen and now were mush. Such variety, I thought. It was what lured you back in spite of yourself.

My first recollection of Juice had been of a little hollow carved in the woods. I'd just quit teaching as a totally artificial exercise – no way of measuring your work, no harvest – and felt quite safe. I still moved, at least in my own mind, inside a protective mantle of authority. Everyone considered my presence on the beach an honor, a social uplift. The country was so barren simply anyone looked good.

A few years must have gone by because the next thing I remember was Adrian's leaving a shop Juice had built in the meantime. My pen pal had just been threatened that if he touched a certain chest the marshal had left, Juice would "fling a wrench through him!" Although Adrian's departing face had been white, his discomfiture had still meant nothing to me. I hadn't known which was funnier, that a lawman would trust a man with Juice's reputation with a valuable chest or that Juice would take the trust so seriously. He was just a nut, one of the sort legends are built around.

Following that fishing season Juice had settled into the role of bonafide neighbor himself. He was now set up to do welding, and in the course of making a dory trailer for me had ignited a synthetic shirt, developing a burn blister on his back the size of a flour sack. Quixotically, I had felt responsible. Now seemed the time to combine my frustrated teaching instincts with something practical, and I tried to get him to see a doctor. Instead, Juice preferred to control his temperature by shuffling around outside in the snow. He had been a familiar figure that winter, lucky not to have been shot for a bear. I always waved or spoke when I went by, but I think it was less from friendship than to salute my luck that he took the pain so calmly. Everyone agreed that luck was something you needed if you lived near Juice.

Like most Alaskans, he was tolerant, but a border had been crossed that night I stopped to nag him for working to all hours. I'd been walking home from a dance at the Community Club and been puzzled by an unusual noise. It had sounded like a grave digger at work in the woods, but finally when I got up courage to call out, I found it was Juice out digging potatoes. At midnight! He even expressed surprise that I should interrupt him, since to him midnight was a time of day.

I hadn't realized at the time that I'd gone too far, any more than Adrian had when he tried to see inside the chest. But it was clear now the residual schoolmaster in me had paved the way for the claim jumping. You did not bring your face too close to a dog's for fear that in that moment he would sense your vulnerability and attack. Paradoxically, I'd been safer on the beach as a newcomer than I was now that I'd proved myself. As Juice's Laplandish structure passed from view – half canvas, half wood

– I understood one of the reasons I always went Outside, or even read when I was here. It was to avoid the inexpressible.

Saying he'd see me tomorrow, Adrian dumped me off at the last spur and spun his car in a circle. As though the situation were rapidly becoming a matter for poets and fools, he seemed in a hurry.

"Thanks a lot!" I said. "It would have been a long walk with all these bags."

"Don't mention it, old buddy. Hope everything turns out all right!"

I watched as the accelerating wheels threw a blast of snow like white chicken feathers in his wake. The ten-mile point marked the limit of official interference with this environment. Except for gray traceries which someone's exhaust had left on the roadside snow, I could see no recent sign of man. There was no hurry now and I didn't hesitate to leave my bags where they sat. I was back, where not even a man like Juice would touch your personal effects. He might steal your wife, but not your rifle. I was even beginning to feel a certain confidence which comes from putting one foot after another uninterrupted under an endless sky, when I noticed a series of prints leading up and over the shelf. I could tell they were old because they looked like bootblacks' shoe supports. It is a principle that when snow is packed, it eventually goes into relief, shedding the softer mold which made it. These inverted boot marks could not have been made last fall, for the erosive action of winter storms would have leveled them. The ambiguous outlook hadn't changed much since I'd gotten off the plane. This was Alaska, all right.

The country had awaited my return a long time. I could tell by the assault on my senses. The ice was unusually rich with the odors of shattered logs, leaves, dead fur. I had stayed on the beach all winter only once and had seen how much it took to produce this little bit of evidence. Dozens of sheets of salt ice had to be driven out of the water by the tide, laminating up to the twenty-foot shelf as it stood. And to make those dusty garden plots on its back the wind had to scour the mud bluff above at a hundred miles an hour, bringing it down particle by frozen particle. At the right moment ice and eroded soil all went away on a few tides. More rapidly than you'd think, they were drawn from the beach just as surely as I hoped the winter's myth would be once the sun developed heat. Today there was still enough chill in the air to blur the vision and grit to make my teeth squeak as I hurried along, scarcely recognizing what was familiar. The cabin roof was a straight line in a slum of icebergs and I was quite close before I saw the broken glass. Too late I realized I'd committed a fundamental error. I'd stumbled into the open like a shrew mouse during a thaw, offering myself as food for the coyotes.

Hoping I still might have the element of surprise, I raced across the porch and ducked under the door for protection. It was locked, but you could step right through the window, shattered as by a bomb blast. The shortcut gave me a criminal's sense of time and space. Inside, the place was surprisingly similar to how I remembered it. Except for some pockets which had been turned inside out, my cold-weather clothes were hanging from nails just as I'd left them. The black numbers on my buoy kegs gave comic expressions to the white end-faces, depending on their rotation. None had been set. The oddest thing in the room was my own fault, consisting of a cascade of dirty nets alive with eyes. On the last day of the season there'd been a big catch of mud flounders that I'd been too tired to pick out. That's how strange you got in September. From then on it was a case of where you were in the scale of evolution. Well, maybe now was the time to find out.

It was only a couple of miles back to Juice's diggings, and I had plenty of nervous energy stored up from the long hours of sitting in planes and airports. To belong to a country you must eat of its flesh, take blows from its trees and its stones, and as I moved through the woods I felt the old affinity returning. Once again Juice and I were breathing the same air.

Back in his dismal dale all seemed tranquil. There was the same acid smell I'd noticed from the road. It was a typical smell of spring. I'd first encountered it one year when my cabin had been occupied by a porcupine. They liked the glue in the cardboard with which I'd lined the walls. Here there were not even droppings. I knew I was breaking a rule by opening the door of the shop, even to the width of the chain, but, faced by the country's gossip, I felt I had a right. Not five feet from me was a large windrow of snow which had formed and was now so big there was no way to get it out. It must have come in a flake at a time, wafted on the wings of those odd woodland breezes that move when it storms. It was the sort of thing that grazed the supernatural and laid the groundwork for the season's fable. Although I would remember my preconceptions of the Alaskan spring chiefly because they were wrong, I doubted that Adrian would. He would go about blindly, occasionally spitting down his dead well, and then wake to the opening day of salmon season as if nothing had happened. Well, I intended to get to the bottom of things, even though it meant breaking and entering. I was about to mark the snow irreparably, when a glimmer of light touched my peripheral vision. It had the acetylene glow of a miner's lamp. Then it went out.

"What can I do for you?" said a voice. There was

no sense in running, so I stepped ahead and let myself be seen.

"I've got something here that needs to be brazed," I said, frantically searching in my old jacket, hoping that the winos who had picked my pockets would have noticed the elbow was faulty. It was off an old carburetor.

"How long have you been here, teacher?" There was still no light, and I thought the voice was wrong. Juice's had been stronger.

"I just got back, Juice."

"So did I." All of a sudden the light flicked on and there was his face, shadow-lit under the lamp. It may have been the illumination, but he was so thin I hardly recognized him. I put the fitting in his hand and he sucked it. It fell off almost immediately. He looked thoughtful.

"I can pick it up later," I offered.

"No need to be in a rush. I've got to see if I have any gas." As though the winter had drained him of his strength, he pawed about his shelves, smelling high and low like a starving dog. At one point I turned away, avoiding his unself-conscious butt decolletage.

"It's been a hard winter," I suggested.

"So I've heard." He must have cut his finger, for he swore. "This damn lamp hasn't worked right since I kicked a man to death in the Usibelli Coal Mine! It would be a hell of a lot easier if I started a power plant for this community. The trouble is no one has any money!"

He found some starting fluid, and, amazingly, the light plant took right off. It sounded like a jackhammer, but I decided to say nothing. If he wanted to be discovered and sent back to jail, that was his business. That assumed there had been a particle of truth in Adrian's story, which I doubted.

There under the cave-like roof of the shelter-well Juice made quick work of the brass fitting, and as soon as it was done, he cancelled out the damning noise. I wanted to get going, but with the confidence of a physician who leaves the finishing touches to a nurse, he put everything away before trying the tiny elbow on his tongue. At first I thought he was trying to control me, but then I saw it was only to give the work time to cool. This time it stuck. He looked pleased.

"How much do I owe you?" I said.

"Nothing neighbor. Next time you bring me a job I'll really barb your ass!"

With Juice's laugh my last remaining doubts dissolved. The flush which came to his face made him look ten years younger. Today, especially, in slacks and sweater which passed with him for best, he resembled the stateside commuters I'd been rubbing elbows with, full of big worries and small troubles. It was time to go.

"Well, thanks a lot," I said.

"Think nothing of it, neighbor. You come back and visit old Juice when you get time. Remember, if you don't I'll be mad!"

I slipped out of his shop and started back across the road. I'd come back a little early, but it would give me time to mend my nets. There was a freshness in this spring that went beyond all imagining. Under such conditions I could easily see myself staying the winter.

I was nearly out of the clearing when I noticed an unusual configuration in the trees. I did not dare change course too much, but from what I could see it definitely was a tractor. Also it had been set on fire. You could see where it was still covered with little twigs which had blotched the yellow paint with soot like the chimney of a poorly trimmed lantern. The branches were withered now as the stems of very old vines. They made a kind of cage over the cylinders. What I couldn't see were the bullet holes and there was no sign of cement. Some might have called such evidence trifling, but I'd been in the museums and knew that the greatest deeds of history left little more in their wake.